Richmond upon Thames Libraries

Renew online at www.richmond.gov.uk/libraries

iLLUSTRATED BY ALEX

D1494510

MEET THE GLOBAL HEROES

MO
ANiMAL SPECiALiST

LiNG
ENVIRONMENTAL EXPERT

KEiRA
TECHNiCiAN

RONAN

MATHS AND PHYSICS EXPERT

FERNANDA

TEAM MEDIC

THE GLOBAL HEROES ARE A GROUP OF CHILDREN FROM AROUND THE WORLD, RECRUITED BY THE MYSTERIOUS BILLIONAIRE, MASON ASH. FROM THE BEEHIVE, THEIR TOP SECRET ISLAND HEADQUARTERS, THEY USE THEIR SPECIAL SKILLS TO HELP PROTECT THE FUTURE OF THE EARTH AND EVERYTHING THAT LIVES ON IT.

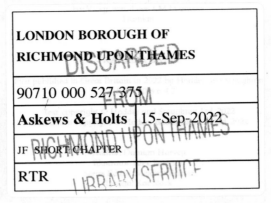
A CIP catalogue record for this book
is available from the British Library.

ISBN 978 1 4451 8095 3 (pbk)
ISBN 978 1 4451 8633 7 (ebook)

Printed and bound in Great Britain by Clays Ltd, St Ives plc

The paper and board used in this book are made from wood from responsible sources.

MIX
Paper from
responsible sources
FSC® C104740

Franklin Watts
An imprint of
Hachette Children's Group
Part of Hodder and Stoughton
Carmelite House
50 Victoria Embankment
London EC4Y 0DZ

An Hachette UK Company
www.hachette.co.uk
www.hachettechildrens.co.uk

CONTENTS

CONTENTS

CHAPTER ONE
A NEW MISSION

Thick clouds of grey smoke filled the air. Flames leapt from tree to tree as a raging fire destroyed everything in its path.

In the living pod of the Beehive, the Global Heroes' top secret headquarters, Mo and Fernanda watched the

devastation on a huge television screen. They'd barely moved a millimetre all day.

Fernanda shook her head. "I feel useless just sitting here watching," she said. "There must be *something* we can do."

Keira looked up from the gadget she was fiddling with. "The professor says we need to wait for the fire teams to get things under control," she told them.

As they watched, a huge Skycrane helicopter flew over the blazing trees and released its load. 3,000 gallons of water dropped onto the bushfire below, extinguishing a large patch of it in a hissing cloud of steam.

Then the image on the television changed to show a news reporter talking to a farmer. The farmer's face and clothes were streaked with dirt and sweat.

They heard how the fire had swept through his home during the night. Luckily, no one was hurt, but all that remained of his farm were piles of twisted metal and smouldering wood.

"That must have been terrifying," said

Fernanda. "*And* he's lost his home."

"It's not only people losing their homes," said Mo. "Just think of all the animals that are losing theirs."

Then, the image on the screen changed again. It showed Mason Ash, sitting in the shadows of his office. Mason was a billionaire whose dream it was to save the planet from environmental disasters. Recruiting young helpers from around the world, Mason had set up the Global Heroes to make that dream come true.

Each of the five young recruits have their own unique abilities. Keira has a passion for technology, while Ronan has a talent for science and maths. Ling cares for the environment. After seeing the damage people do to the world she's determined to make a change. Fernanda's mother is a doctor, and her father a vet. She's always ready to put the medical knowledge she's gained from them to good use. Mo is the newest recruit. He wants to help endangered animals, and with the Global Heroes he gets to do just that.

"Good morning, everyone," said Mason.

"Good morning, Mason," the three friends replied, eager to hear what he had to say.

"Have you seen the bushfire?" Fernanda quickly asked.

"That's why I'm contacting you now," Mason replied.

"A mission!" cried Mo, excitedly.

Mason had only just recruited Mo and it was clear how eager he was to go on a mission. Fernanda smiled. She remembered how excited she'd been to go on her first Global Heroes mission.

"What do you want us to do?" she asked. "Help put out the fires?"

"No!" Mason replied. "That's a job for the professionals. Your task will be to help locate and rescue any wildlife still left there."

"Great!" said Keira, waving her new gadget. "I'll be able to test this. It can detect living things from their body heat. It can even detect things that are underground."

"That'll be useful," said Mason. "But *you'll* have to wait until Ling and Ronan get back to the Beehive. We need at least one of you here to keep an eye on things."

Keira sighed, but reluctantly agreed.

"Don't worry," Fernanda told her.

"You can join up with us later using your GPS tracker."

Keira grinned. She loved any chance she could get to use a gadget. "Just make sure you keep your rucksacks with you at all times," she said. "The tracker chips are sewn into them."

"There's just one more thing," said Mason. "I have a feeling you might not be alone ... so keep your wits about you and your eyes open."

Mo looked puzzled but Fernanda knew what Mason meant. "Evilooters!" she said.

"What are Evilooters?" asked Mo.

"You mean *who* are Evilooters?" replied Keira. "We'll tell you about them later. We'd better not keep Professor Darwin waiting."

The aqua lift at the centre of the Beehive carried the friends up to the landing pod where they would meet up with the professor.

"I still can't believe this is water powered," said Mo.

"Everything in the Beehive is environmentally friendly," Keira reminded him. "We can't go around

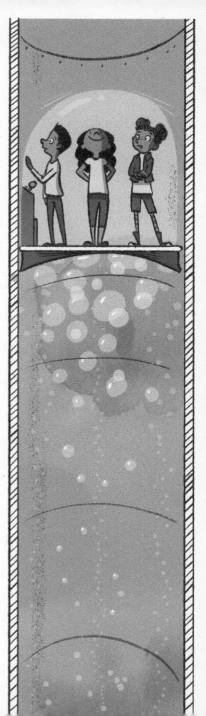

trying to save the planet if we're polluting it too."

As the lift doors slid open, Fernanda pulled a face. "Speaking of pollution," she said. "What's that awful smell?"

"It's not me," said Mo, covering his nose.

"It's coming from up there," said Keira, pointing to a platform up above where they could see Professor Darwin peering into a large storage tank.

As they crossed the floor the professor spotted them and gave a wave. "I'll be right with you," she called.

"What's that awful smell?" asked Keira.

"My latest invention," said the professor, proudly.

"You've invented a bad smell?" asked Mo.

"It's an organic fuel processor," she replied. "It converts waste matter into highly efficient fuel for the eco-boosters. Leftover food and other waste goes in, and environmentally friendly fuel comes out."

"It sounds great," said Fernanda.

"It *smells* terrible," added Mo.

The professor paused and took a deep breath. "No!" she said. "It smells natural. Now, your eco-booster is fuelled and ready and your rucksacks are on board."

As the roof of the landing pod slid open above them, Professor Darwin explained

that the destination coordinates were set. "You can just sit back and enjoy the flight," she said. "Keira and I will keep an eye on you from the control pod."

Fernanda and Mo clambered into the cockpit of the eco-booster, fastened their safety belts and put their helmets on.

Mo grinned and gave a thumbs up.

"Okay," said Fernanda. "We're ready."

The eco-booster rose into the air with hardly a sound. Mo watched as the

Global Heroes' headquarters grew smaller beneath them. Made up from hexagonal shaped pods, it was easy to see why the building had been given its name. From above, it did look a bit like a beehive.

"Good luck," came Professor Darwin's voice in their helmets. "The world clock is counting. You've got forty-eight hours to complete your mission."

CHAPTER TWO
LANDING IN AUSTRALIA

Fernanda hadn't realised she'd fallen asleep until a voice in her headset woke her up.

"I've located a safe landing area," said Professor Darwin. "In five minutes you'll touch down on the east coast of

Australia."

Fernanda yawned. "That didn't take long," she said.

Mo laughed. "You've been asleep for ages," he said. "And you were supposed to be telling me about the Evilooters."

"Sorry!" said Fernanda. "I always fall asleep on flights."

"I don't know how anyone can sleep when the world is whizzing by their window," said Mo.

The faint sound coming from the eco-booster's thrusters changed slightly, indicating that they were coming in to land. As the craft descended, clouds of smoke made it almost impossible to see anything outside.

★ ★ ★

Mo was starting to feel nervous. He could feel his heart beating a little faster as smoke surrounded them.

"Don't worry," Fernanda assured him. "You'll be fine."

"How far from the fire will we be?" Mo asked.

"The fire's out where you are," came the professor's voice. "But as you can see, there's still lots of smoke so you're going to have to be careful."

Mo nodded. "I hope we'll be able to

locate the stranded animals," he said.

Professor Darwin told them that the air should be clearer once they were on the ground, and she was right. As the eco-booster gently touched down, they got their first view of the devastation caused by the fires.

A mixture of steam and smoke rose up from the ground and all around them were the charred remains of trees and bushes. Fire crews were busy rolling up hoses, their yellow helmets streaked with smoke and soot.

How could anything survive this? Mo wondered.

Fernanda was clambering down from the eco-booster when Professor Darwin's voice chirped in her headset again. "Your contact is leading firefighter Scotty Wilson. He'll direct you from there."

"Thanks, Professor," she replied.

"Don't forget this," Mo called, passing Fernanda's rucksack down to her. "Keira said we should keep them on at all times."

Fernanda slung the rucksack onto her back and made her way towards one of the firefighters. She didn't know what their contact looked like, but she could see the name Scotty, written on the back of his helmet.

As she approached, the firefighter turned and raised his visor. "There you are," he said with a friendly smile. "That flying machine of yours is quiet. I didn't hear a thing."

"No fuel pollution and no noise pollution either," said Fernanda. "It's one hundred per cent environmentally friendly."

"It's great you could join us," said the firefighter. "The rangers need all the help they can get."

Scotty showed Mo and Fernanda a map of the area and pointed out a large cross. "That's the rescue centre for injured animals," he said. "The only problem is finding them all. That's where you come in."

"We'll find as many as we can," said Mo.

Scotty pointed towards what had once been a path into the bush.

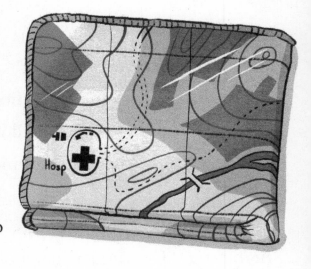

"If you head that way," he said, "you should come across the rest of the search team."

Fernanda thanked Scotty and started to make her way along the path.

"Wait for me!" cried Mo, struggling to get his rucksack on.

The smell of smoke filled the air and the ground was warm beneath their feet.

Even though the fire had been put out, everything around them felt hot.

★ ★ ★

They walked in silence for a while, carefully making their way past burnt trees and bushes. There was no sign of the rest of the search party, or of any wildlife. It was like walking in another world. A world without any life.

Then all of a sudden, something caught Mo's eye.

"Wait," he whispered, sure that he had seen something move.

Fernanda stopped and looked back at him. "What is it?" she asked.

Mo stood perfectly still.

"Up there," he whispered, looking at the remains of a eucalyptus tree. High up in its scorched branches sat two koalas, clutching the tree trunk and staring down at them.

"What are we going to do?" Fernanda whispered.

Mo thought for a moment. Koalas are easily frightened. He knew they should be left alone – but this was an emergency. The fire had destroyed their home. They had nowhere to live and nothing to eat.

"Don't make any sudden movements," Mo whispered. "And be as quiet as you can."

Very slowly, they made their way towards the tree. Before they reached it, Mo stopped. He knew koalas didn't like people to touch the tree they were sitting in and he felt unsure about what to do next.

Luckily, the female koala knew exactly what to do.

She scrambled down from the tree and came towards them, her paws held out. Fernanda crouched down and the koala came straight to her.

"That's lucky," said Mo. "Perhaps they're used to seeing people."

Mo crouched down and picked up the bigger, male koala when it came to him.

"They must know we only want to help," said Fernanda.

"I can't believe how well that went," said Mo.

The words had just left his lips when Fernanda let out a little gasp. "Look!" she whispered.

Mo turned to see another, smaller koala coming down from the higher branches of the tree.

"They had a joey!" said Mo. "I should have thought of that."

The frightened joey took one look at Mo and Fernanda and ran. The two of them watched helplessly as it disappeared into the smoky remains of the forest.

CHAPTER THREE
LOST AND FOUND

Back at the Beehive, Keira had been
pacing up and down, waiting for Ling
and Ronan to get back from their
mission. As soon as the team's eco-booster
touched down, Keira was desperate to

set off to join Mo and Fernanda, but Professor Darwin made her wait.

The professor insisted on running safety checks on the eco-booster before allowing it to take off again. "And it needs refuelling," she told Keira.

As soon as the professor gave the all-clear, Keira was strapping herself into the eco-booster's cockpit. "Sorry!" she said to Ling and Ronan. "I really do want to hear how your mission went ... as soon as I get back."

After a quick wave goodbye, Keira's eco-booster blasted off. It wasn't long before she was high above the South Pacific Ocean, speeding towards the east coast of Australia.

Every few minutes she glanced down at her GPS tracker. Two green triangles showed where Fernanda and Mo were. She couldn't wait to join them.

Even though they had only left their top secret headquarters an hour or so before her, it had seemed much longer.

★ ★ ★

Down on the ground, Mo and Fernanda stood side by side with the two koalas clinging on to them. Mo peered between the smouldering trees and piles of ash, looking for anything that might show which way the baby koala had gone.

"It's hard to see anything with all this smoke," he said. "I think the wind's blowing it towards us."

Fernanda nodded. "It's making my eyes sting," she said. "Perhaps we should head towards the rescue centre with these two koalas."

"But we can't just leave the little joey behind," Mo insisted.

"I know," said Fernanda, "but we can't risk getting lost in the smoke either. We have to think of our own safety too."

Mo reluctantly agreed. "Which way is it?" he asked.

A worried look crossed Fernanda's face. "I'm not sure," she said. "Everything looks the same."

"I think the path is back that way," said Mo, sounding uncertain.

They were about to set off when the sound of a muffled voice reached their ears.

"Hello! Hello!" came the voice. "Mo?

Fernanda? Are you there?"

"Your radio!" cried Fernanda. "That's Keira's voice."

"The radio's in my rucksack," said Mo. He turned round so that Fernanda could look for it without putting the koala down.

"Here it is," she said, pressing her thumb against the "talk" button. "Keira!" she said. "Where are you?"

"I've just landed," replied Keira. "I was going to come and meet you but it looks like you had better come to me."

"That's a great idea," said Fernanda. "There's just one problem … I think we're lost."

"I can see you on my GPS tracker," said Keira. "It looks like you're heading north-west at the moment. You just need to change course slightly. I'm west of where you are now."

Mo checked his compass and pointed. "That way," he said. The two of them set off between the trees, keeping a careful hold on the koalas. The smoke seemed to be thinning out a little.

Mo's radio crackled to life again and Keira confirmed that they were heading in the right direction. "You should find yourself at the edge of a clearing pretty soon," she said. "I'm in the middle of it."

Keira was right. After going a few more metres, walking became easier. They could see that the ground had been cleared of fallen branches and tree trunks. The air was clearer too. Up ahead they spotted Fernanda waving to them.

"What happened here?" asked Mo, looking at the clearing.

Keira explained that the area they were in had been cleared by the fire teams

earlier in the week. She said one way of stopping a bushfire spreading to another area was to set a controlled fire.

Fernanda nodded. "I've heard about

that," she said. "It's called prescribed burning. They do it to make a firebreak."

"I see," said Mo. "So the bushfire can't get past here because there's nothing left to burn."

While they had been talking, the koala that was holding on to Fernanda had started making a grunting sound.

"What's wrong with it?" asked Keira.

"She's a koala and she's frightened, " said Fernanda.

Soon, the male koala put his head back and starting grunting too. "Their little joey is still out in the bush," said Mo.

"He ran away before we could rescue him."

"I can help," said Keira, excitedly. She reached into her rucksack and took out the new gadget she'd been fiddling with at the Beehive. "We should be able to locate the joey with this."

As soon as Keira turned the new gadget on, it started making a high-pitched beeping sound. Keira turned the volume level down and stared at the screen. As she looked, a worried expression crossed her face.

"What is it?" asked Fernanda.

Keira held the gadget up so they could both see the screen. "That's us," she said, indicating three green triangles at the bottom of the screen.

Mo frowned. "What about all those red triangles?" he asked.

"Evilooters!" said Keira. "Lots of them … and they're heading right for us."

CHAPTER FOUR
KOALA RESCUE

"This way," urged Fernanda. "We need to get out of here."

Keira agreed and began following Fernanda across the clearing, but Mo didn't move. He stood with a determined look on his face, holding the koala close to him.

"Come on!" Fernanda urged. "Don't just stand there."

Mo shook his head. "No!" he said. "Not until you tell me about these Evilooters."

Fernanda let out a frustrated sigh. "There's no time right now," she insisted.

"There no time like the present," said Mo. "That's what Professor Darwin says. If you don't do something when you can, you might not get another chance."

Fernanda let out another sigh. "If we don't get going, the Evilooters will capture these koalas."

Mo didn't understand. "Why would they do that?" he asked.

"So they can sell them," said Fernanda. "The Evilooters are only interested in making money, and they don't care how much damage they do to the environment while they're doing it."

"In that case," said Mo.,"we need to do something about them."

"He's right," said Keira."But we need to make a plan."

Mo was determined that the first thing they should do was find the missing joey. "We don't want it falling into the hands of the Evilooters."

As they talked, the female koala Fernanda was carrying started to wriggle and squirm. She tried to get it to settle

EVILOOTER CHARACTERS

EVILOOTER BIKER

DECEPTION: 40

POLLUTING LEVEL: 50

CUNNING: 40

GREED: 65

ENVIRONMENTAL THREAT: 49

down, but it was no use. The koala was
determined to get free. With a final
wriggle, she dropped to the ground and
started heading back towards the burnt
remains of the bush. Back towards the
Evilooters.

The male koala let out a bellowing
grunt as he slid out of Mo's arms and
dropped to the ground too. With their
short legs, koalas aren't well adapted for
running and Mo was surprised at how
quickly they bounded across the clearing.
"Stop them!" he cried.

"Wait," said Keira. "Perhaps we should
see where they're going."

"She's right," said Fernanda. "They might lead us to the joey."

Mo was concerned they might have trouble finding the koalas again if they lost sight of them, but Keira said not to worry.

She knew they would be able
to keep track of them on her new
tracking device.

Fernanda and Mo gathered round as
Keira pointed at the coloured triangles
on the screen. The red triangles of the
Evilooters were near the middle
of the screen.

They were a little too close for comfort,
but at least they didn't seem to be moving.

"I wonder what
they're up to,"
said Keira.
"Perhaps
they have
a camp,"
suggested
Mo.

"Perhaps," Fernanda replied. "But I don't trust them."

The friends could also see two little blue triangles on the screen.

"That's them," said Keira, tapping the screen. "Your two koalas."

"And there's the joey," Mo cried excitedly, as another blue triangle appeared.

"It could be," said Keira. "Though it could be something else. A wombat perhaps, or maybe a baby kangaroo."

"No!" said Mo. "It's the joey. I know it is."

If it was the little joey, it could soon be in trouble. He was getting dangerously

close to the Evilooters. "Come on!" Fernanda urged. "We have to rescue that joey."

They hadn't gone far when they spotted the two adult koalas ahead of them. They were clinging to the burnt remains of a tree and calling out with little grunts and barks.

In the distance, they could hear the faint squeaks and cries of the little joey answering.

But then there was something else too.

The gentle breeze that had carried the smell of smoke towards them earlier on now carried another smell through the air. The foul stench of diesel fumes, and with it, the sound of a revving engine.

Keira looked down at the tracking device and let out a groan.

"One of the Evilooters is heading this way," she said. "They must have heard the koalas."

"We'd better turn back," said Fernanda.

"Not yet!" said Mo. "Look! There's the little joey."

Up ahead they could see the baby koala heading towards them across the burnt ground.

The adult koalas had seen the joey too. They were eager to reach it, but the sound of the motorbike was frightening the timid creatures. They both turned and headed back towards the clearing.

The noise of the engine was getting louder with every second. They couldn't see the motorbike yet, but a plume of exhaust smoke, dirt and dust, rose into the air as it headed in their direction.

"Even if the joey reaches its parents,

that Evilooter will easily catch the koalas in the clearing," said Keira.

"In that case we need to stop the Evilooter before it gets there," said Fernanda, taking off her rucksack. "Perhaps I have something in here that'll help."

CHAPTER FiVE
SETTiNG A TRAP

While Fernanda frantically rooted in
her rucksack, Keira kept a lookout. In
the distance she could just make out the
flickering shape of a motorbike and rider
as it steadily weaved its way between
burnt-out trees and branches.

Time was running out —
it would be next to them in a couple
of minutes.

The team's rucksacks were supposed to
hold everything needed for a mission. But
so far, Fernanda couldn't find anything of
use. Apart from some sandwiches, a bottle
of water, and a spare battery for her
phone, most of the bag was taken up with
medical supplies.

"There must be something!" she cried,
pulling out rolls of bandages to see what
lay underneath.

"Bandages!" cried Mo. "We can use
those."

Fernanda looked at him blankly, but

as Mo quickly explained what he had in mind, a huge grin spread across her face. "Will it work?" she asked.

Mo shrugged. "There's only one way to find out."

They each grabbed a handful of tightly rolled bandages and ran back towards the clearing. At the end of the path stood a couple of large tree trunks that had escaped the worst of the fire. As quickly as they could, the three friends tied long lengths of bandage around one of the trunks. Then, stretching the bandages out, they tied the other ends around the

other tree. Mo hoped that the Evilooter
would ride between the tree trunks
before spotting them. As they stepped
back into the clearing, Mo saw that the
little joey had reached its parents. He
wanted to go and make sure that it was
all right, but at that moment the noise
from the Evilooter's bike became almost

deafening.

Mo turned in time
to see it speeding
towards them
through the bush.
Chains fitted to the
bike's tyres dug into
the ground and sent
earth flying into
the air behind it.
The leather-clad
rider grinned as he
swung a large net
around in the air
above his head – a
net that Mo guessed

was intended to catch animals.

The three friends just had time to jump out of the way as the bike raced between the two tree trunks where they had tied the bandages. The look on the rider's face suddenly changed to one of surprise as the bandages caught around his chest and sent him crashing to the ground. The huge motorbike carried on without him for a few metres, then crashed into a large boulder.

"You make sure the rider isn't too badly hurt," said Keira. "I'm going to look at that bike. I've never seen anything like it before."

The Evilooter lay on the floor,

groaning and rubbing his chest. He glared at Fernanda and Mo as they peered down at him. "You'll pay for that, you meddling kids," he growled. "I'll see that you do."

"He seems fine to me," said Mo. "But let's get going before any more of them turn up."

Keira told them that the Evilooter's bike would be out of action for a while. "That should give us time to get away," she said. "But first, I want to send these pictures to Ronan to look at."

While Keira contacted Ronan back at the Beehive, Mo and Fernanda went to look for the koalas.

They found them huddled together, the

joey fast asleep.

"We need to get them to the rescue centre as soon as possible," said Mo.

"They've been under a lot of stress and that can put their lives at risk."

★ ★ ★

After locating the rescue centre with her GPS tracker, Keira led the way into the bush at the other side of the clearing. The little joey was holding on tight to his mother, so it was down to Mo and Fernanda to carry the koalas between them.

As they walked, Keira spoke to Ronan back at the Beehive. They were all keen to hear what he had discovered so she switched her phone on to loudspeaker.

"I've been scanning the internet for information about those motorbikes," Ronan told them. "It seems that someone has been building and selling high-carbon-emitting motorbikes. They consume twice as much fuel as eco-friendly bikes and emit dangerous levels of pollutants into the atmosphere."

"Bikes like that will increase global warming," added Ling. "They're illegal."

"But that doesn't stop people making or buying them," said Ronan. "And I think we can guess who's behind it all."

Keira nodded. "Evilooters," she replied.

CHAPTER SIX
THE CHASE

By the time they reached the Rescue Centre, Fernanda, Keira and Mo had the feeling that their mission was far from over. Mo and Fernanda had grown attached to the koalas and couldn't help feeling sad to be parting with them.

"Don't worry," Dr Goonan, the head vet at the rescue centre, assured them. "They really are in the best place.

We'll take care of them now."

Mo nodded as one of the vet's assistants took the sleeping koala from him. "I know," he replied. "It's just that ... you know."

Dr Goonan smiled. "Believe me, letting them go never gets any easier," he said. "But you've all done a great job."

Mo grinned. "Thanks," he said. "We appreciate that."

"And you're welcome to come back and see how the little guys are getting along," Dr Goonan added.

None of them had a chance to say anything else. The doors to the rescue centre swung open and more injured animals were brought in.

"Can I have some help with these kangaroos?" Dr Goonan called.

Mo was about to step forwards but Fernanda put her hand on his arm to stop

him. "Not us," she said. "We've got other things to do."

"What do you mean?" asked Mo.

"We need to stop the Evilooters," said Fernanda.

Ronan had told them that Mason Ash, the head of Global Heroes, had already been in touch with the Australian authorities. The police were ready to arrest the Evilooters, but it was down to Fernanda, Keira and Mo to get the villains to them.

"How are we going to do that?" asked Mo.

"It's funny you should ask," said Keira. "I've got an idea."

As Keira explained her plan for rounding up the Evilooters, Mo began to look more and more worried. He didn't like the sound of walking into their camp and he certainly didn't like the sound of getting the Evilooters to chase them.

"They'll catch us straight away," said Mo. "We can't outrun their motorbikes."

Keira smiled. "While you were talking to Dr Goonan, I was arranging things," she said. "And the first was transport."

"Cool!" said Mo. "What have we got?"

"Eco-friendly dirt bikes?" said Fernanda, hopefully.

"What about four-wheel drive eco-friendly quad bikes?" said Mo.

"Our transport is totally eco-friendly," said Keira. "And it's waiting outside."

Mo and Fernanda could hardly wait. Waving to Dr Goonan, they dashed out of the rescue centre.

Lying on the floor were three old mountain bikes. They were covered with scratches, dents and dried-on mud.

"Not as fast as the Evilooters' motorbikes," said Fernanda. "But much more friendly to the environment."

"And," said Keira, "we should be able to use some paths that the Evilooters can't manage on their huge motorbikes."

The mountain bikes had wide tyres to stop them sinking into the dusty ground. Pedalling was hard work, but it was faster than walking, and before long, the three friends spotted the Evilooters' camp.

They got off their bikes and crept closer to get a better look. Then they saw the Evilooters' motorbikes, covered over with camouflaged netting.

"It's no wonder the police helicopter has trouble finding them," said Keira. "But they shouldn't have any problem seeing that big truck."

"Perhaps that isn't normally here," said Fernanda. "I wonder what they're doing?"

As they watched, Evilooters began loading large crates on to the truck. Fernanda took out her phone and edged closer. "I want to get this on video," she said. "It's evidence."

Mo was wondering what was in
the crates when one of the Evilooters
suddenly dropped one. The crate broke
and something ran out. "A kangaroo!" he
cried, as it hopped away.

Keira had been busy looking at her
tracking gadget. "What is it?" she asked.

"They're not just crates," said Mo. "They're cages."

A sudden shout came up from the Evilooters' camp and Fernanda came racing back towards them. "I've been spotted!" she cried, jumping on to her mountain bike.

With Keira taking the lead, the three of them raced off together. "Follow me!" she shouted.

They had only gone a short distance when they heard the thundering roar of engines.

"They're coming!" cried Mo.

"I never thought getting them to follow us would be that easy," Fernanda admitted.

"Well you did film them stealing wild animals," said Mo, pedalling as fast as he could.

As they dodged and weaved their way between fallen branches and burnt trees, they could hear roaring motorbikes behind them. Keira had been right … the mountain bikes could fit between small gaps. But the Evilooters just smashed through everything in their path.

"They're gaining on us," shouted Mo.

"Nearly there!" shouted Keira.

Fernanda looked back over her shoulder and immediately wished she hadn't. The Evilooters were right behind

them.

Suddenly, something sharp stabbed at her arm – a broken tree branch.

She let out a cry of pain and the bike wobbled beneath her, almost making her fall off.

Mo could feel his leg muscles burning with the effort of pedalling. He knew the Evilooters were right behind but he didn't dare look back. After ducking his head to avoid some overhanging branches, he looked up to find they had entered a large clearing. And they weren't alone.

Behind him, the Evilooters came to a skidding halt when they found themselves

facing a line of police cars, their lights flashing.

"We've done it!" said Mo, with a huge grin on his face. "Mission accomplished."

But his grin soon faded when he saw Fernanda and Keira, both shaking their heads.

"Not yet it's not," said Fernanda. "But that's enough for today."

CHAPTER SEVEN
NO MORE BUSHFIRES

Back at the Beehive, Ronan and Ling excitedly buzzed their friends, Fernanda, Keira and Mo.

"Guess what, you are going to spend the night in a luxury cabin on a dairy farm," Ronan cried excitedly down the radio. "Mason has arranged everything."

"High View Farm is far away from the fire zone," Ling explained, "so you will be safe there, but can recover and help the local community at the same time."

"That sounds awesome!" Fernanda, Mo and Keira agreed.

In what felt like no time, Keira, Mo, and Fernanda arrived outside a farm that was set amongst lush trees and bush, without a flame or sooty smoke cloud in sight.

"Welcome to High View," said Mike, vigorously shaking the friends' hands. "I'm

Mike and this is my wife, Melissa."

As they made their way down to the log cabin, Mike told them that their eco-boosters were stored safely in one of the barns. "We knew they were coming," he said. "But it was still strange seeing them landing on their own like that."

"It's even stranger when you're on board," said Keira. "But you do get used to it. Professor Darwin flies them remotely from the Beehive. It's good to know they're in a safe place."

The three friends wanted to find out

what had been causing the bushfires. Maybe they could help prevent them in the future. Luckily, the cabin had laptops they could use – and a good internet connection. There was also a huge map of Australia on the wall.

Back at the Beehive, Ling, the environmental expert in the team, had been busy doing research. She had been learning about forest and bushfires – especially those in Australia. Ling and Ronan video-called to tell them what she had discovered.

"First, you need to know that most bushfires are started by accident. Sometimes by humans," Ling said.

"Like a campfire or barbecue getting out of control. But more are caused by lightning."

"Wait a minute," said Mo. "I thought it rained when there was lightning. Wouldn't that put the fires out?"

"Not always," said Ling. She explained to them that some fires became so big and so hot that the rainwater evaporated before reaching the ground. This resulted in what was known as dry lightning. She also told them about firestorms – fires that were so intense that they created their own wind.

"Does this mean that the Evilooters aren't to blame for this latest fire?" asked

Fernanda.

Ronan told them that they weren't sure about that yet as they hadn't identified where the fire started. "They might not be responsible for that, but they contribute to the bigger problem: burning fossil fuels."

"That's right, Ronan," Ling continued. She had discovered that the fires were made worse by global warming and changes in weather. Fires were starting more frequently, burning for longer and spreading much faster.

"Once fires get started they need two things to keep them going," said Ling. "Heat and fuel."

Ling also said that global warming was causing an increase in something known as fire weather.

"What's fire weather?" asked Keira.

"It's a combination of things that cause an increased risk of fire," Ling told her. "First, an increase in air temperature,

combined with low humidity and a lack
of rain, dries out the vegetation. Dry
grass, trees and bushes make great fuel for
a fire. Wind speed
and direction can help the fire spread
faster too."

Keira shook her head with concern.
"So if we don't stop
global warming,
there'll be an
increase in
fire weather,"
she said.

"That's
right," Ling
replied.

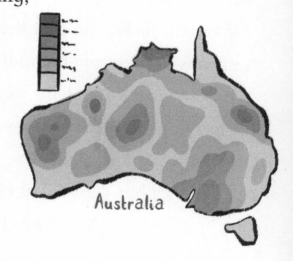

Australia

"Bushfires or wildfires could become a lot more common in Australia, as well as in other countries around the world."

Listening to Ling explain things, it became clear that environmental problems often had connections with each other. As one thing got worse, so did something else — like droughts and the increased risk of fire.

Mo got the feeling that the more missions he went on, the more he would see how Earth's problems were connected. "I just hope that the work we do will help the planet in some way."

"That's what the Global Heroes are for," said Keira. "We get to the bottom of

these issues and spread the word on how to stop them and make a difference."

"It can start with us," cried Fernanda,

"but I am sure more people will join in to help preserve our planet for the future. For now let's get some rest, we have a busy day tomorrow."

CHAPTER EIGHT
PLANTING TREES

"Morning, sleepyheads," came a loud, cheerful voice. "It's time you were up and ready."

They had barely had time to gather their things together when Mike Jones put his head round the door. "You guys ready?" he asked. "We've got work to do."

After piling into the back of Mike's truck, Melissa told them what they had planned for the day. A few kilometres away was an area of land that had been badly burnt in a fire the year before. Local volunteers were working together to plant new trees. "We thought you might like to see how it's going," she said.

The three friends expected the ground to look black and burned but what they saw came as a surprise. There was only a scattering of trees and bushes, some still showing signs of damage, but the ground itself was green.

And everywhere they looked there were volunteers busy planting trees.

"It depends how bad the fires are, but seeds and roots can survive," Mike told them. "That means some things start to grow back quickly. Trees like the eucalyptus take a lot longer."

"But eucalyptus trees are vital for wildlife," said Mo. "Creatures like sugar gliders and koalas depend on them. As well as giving them somewhere to live, it also gives them food. They eat the leaves and the sugar gliders even drink the sap."

"That's right," Melissa said. "Without the trees, they will die out."

"So what can we do?" asked Fernanda.

"You can help by planting a tree," Mike said, leading them to a large tent. Inside were wooden tables, all covered with little plant pots. Inside each pot was a small sapling.

"All of these saplings have come from seeds that were grown right here," he said. "So it's like they're coming home again."

After being shown what to do, they spent an hour digging little holes and planting more trees.

"Wow, my back's really aching," complained Keira.

"Mine too," said Mo. "But just think – for the forest and the creatures that live here, each tree you plant is one step towards recovery."

It was soon time to head back to High

View Farm, but Mike and Melissa had
one more surprise. There was just time
to call in at the rescue centre where they
had left the family of koalas.

Dr Goonan was delighted to see them.
And so, it seemed, was the little joey. As
soon as it spotted Fernanda and Mo, it let
out an excited squeak and held its arms

out towards them.

"Now that is a surprise," said the vet, with a grin. "He must really trust you." They were delighted to hear that the koalas were doing well and that they'd soon be ready to move to a new home. But now it was time for Fernanda, Keira and Mo to return to the Beehive. As they left Dr Goonan and the koalas behind, the eco-boosters were just landing outside.

"Professor Darwin thought it'd be quicker to bring them here for you," Mike told them. "She said something about the world clock ticking ..."

"Forty-eight hours!" cried Keira. "We only had forty-eight hours to complete the mission."

Mo frowned. "What if time runs out?" he asked.

Fernanda and Keira looked at each other and shrugged. "We don't know," they agreed. "And we don't want to find out."

"Well, what are you waiting for?" said Mo, running towards the eco-boosters. "Let's go."

Back at the Beehive, Professor Darwin, Ronan and Ling were waiting as the two eco-boosters touched down in the landing pod. The face of Mason Ash looked down from a large television screen on the wall.

"Well done all of you," said Mason. "And especially you, Mo ... how does it feel to have completed your first mission?"

Mo tried his best to smile, but something was bothering him. "It was good," he replied. "I guess."

Mason frowned. "You only guess?" he said. "I hear it was a great success."

"But we only managed to rescue one family of koalas," said Mo. "I'd hoped that we would rescue much more than that."

Mason smiled. "You did save more than that," he said. "And you stopped the Evilooters."

"If you hadn't stopped them," said

Professor Darwin, "hundreds of other wild animals would have been captured and sold."

What Mason Ash and Professor Darwin were saying made perfect sense. They had rescued lots of creatures, but there was still something bothering Mo.

He couldn't quite put his finger on what it was.

Then he had it. The countdown clock on the wall was still ticking. "But if our mission was such a success," said Mo, "why is the world clock still ticking?"

Everyone looked at the huge clock, its minute hand counting out the seconds.

Mason Ash let out a sigh. "The world clock never stops," he said. "There's always another mission – and I think this next one could be your toughest yet."

The friends all looked at each other, then gathered round to hear what Mason Ash had to say next.

THE END

COUNTRY PROFILE:

FAST FACTS:

✱Australia is a large island that lies between the Indian and Pacific Ocean

✱It is the 6th largest country in the world

AUSTRALIA

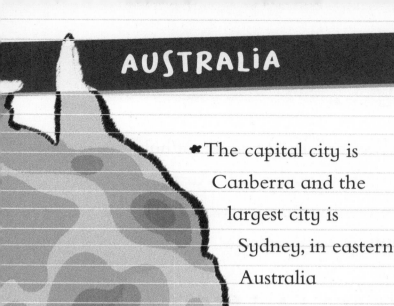

* The capital city is Canberra and the largest city is Sydney, in eastern Australia

* It is part of a continent called Oceania

* Nearly one third of Australia is covered by deserts

* It is home to the Great Barrier Reef, the largest collection of coral reefs on Earth

FACT SHEET:

There are a huge range of habitats, plants and animals native to Australia. Koalas and kangaroos are two of the most famous native species.

KOALA FAST FACTS:

* They are not bears, they are marsupials (they have pouches where they can carry their babies, just like kangaroos)

* Their main diet is eucalyptus leaves

* They hug trees in summer to keep cool

* They spend most of their day asleep

AUSTRALIA

KANGAROO FAST FACTS:

* Kangaroos are the largest marsupials on Earth

* Some can hop up to 7.5 metres

* They can reach speeds of up to 56 km per hour using their large hind legs and powerful tail

* A group of kangaroos is called a mob

* Kangaroos eat grass, herbs and shrubs

* They are great at swimming – and boxing!

Bushfires or wildfires occur when the weather is hot and dry. They are more frequent because the world is getting hotter due to climate change.

CAUSE:

When the weather has been very hot and dry, it creates the perfect conditions for a fire. The hotter it is, the easier for things to catch on fire as there is no moisture in the ground.

Wind can help to spread the fire too, by providing the oxygen which helps fires to burn. When the wind changes direction, a fire covers a greater area, making it very difficult to stop.

BUSHFIRES

EFFECT:

Large areas of forest are lost to fires, meaning people's and animals' homes are destroyed, and sources of food for animals becomes much harder to find, too.

It's not all negative, though:

* Some trees, such as eucalyptus, only release their seeds when they feel the heat of a fire

* When fire clears the undergrowth, new plants can grow – the ash left by fires acts as a fertiliser for the plants

* The new plants provide food for animals, as well as new shelter and places to live

FACT SHEET:

The world is getting warmer and weather more extreme because of human activity.

It's not too late to help look after the planet.

Little steps can make a big difference …

Join the Global Heroes in their mission to protect Earth's future. Here are some ideas, but there are plenty more!

CLIMATE ACTION

1) Write a poem, story or news article about bushfires to make people aware of them

2) Make a poster about climate changes to share with your class at school

3) Find out about local community projects, such as:

* a local litter pick
* helping to plant some local trees

4) Travel by public transport or bike, walk or scoot when possible

5) Try to reuse and recycle as much as you can

6) Don't waste food – use leftovers to make another tasty dish

QUIZ

1) What is the name for a baby koala?

2) What does a koala eat?

3) What can cause a bushfire?

4) What is a firebreak?

5) Which other animal is at the rescue centre?

6) Which creatures live in eucalyptus trees?

7) What activity do the team do that helps offset climate change?

(Answers 1. Joey; 2. Eucalyptus leaves; 3. Hot, dry weather; 4. A way of stopping burning; 5. Kangaroos; 6. Koalas and Sugar Gliders; 7. Planting new trees)

GLOSSARY

ASH – the leftover waste when something is burned

BUSHFIRE – a fire in a forest

CLEARING – an open space in a forest

COCKPIT – where the pilot sits in an aircraft

COMPASS – an instrument used to work out direction

DEVASTATION – the ruins that are left after a disaster

EUCALYPTUS – an evergreen tree, common in Australia

FiREBREAK – something used to stop a fire from spreading

FUEL – coal, gas, or oil used to power things

GPS – short for Global Positioning System, a way of locating where you are

HEADQUARTERS – the base or centre of an organisation

JOEY – baby koala or kangaroo

MARSUPIAL – mammal that has a pouch to carry its young

POLLUTION – harmful materials

SOOT – black powder from burning

VISOR – see-through part of a helmet

WILDLIFE – animals or plants that live in the wild

WOMBAT – small mammal native to Australia

READ
WAVES OF WASTE

TO FIND OUT WHAT MISSION MO, FERNANDA, KEIRA, RONAN AND LING ARE ON NEXT!

GLOBAL HEROES

JOIN THE GLOBAL HEROES TEAM IN THESE FANTASTIC ADVENTURES:

9781445180953

9781445182988

9781445182964

9781445182971